Ask and it will be given to you; seek and you will find;
knock and the door will be opened to you.

—Matthew 7:7

The Berenstain Bears Say Their Prayers

Requests for information should be addressed to:
Zonderkidz, *Grand Rapids, Michigan 49530*

Library of Congress Cataloging-in-Publication Data

Berenstain, Michael.
The Berenstain Bears say their prayers / created by Stan and Jan Berenstain ; written by Mike Berenstain.
p. cm.
Summary: When Brother sees his cousin Fred praying before their baseball game, he decides to give it a try, but he is disappointed when he strikes out anyway.
ISBN-13: 978-0-310-71246-6 (softcover)
ISBN-10: 0-310-71246-7 (softcover)
[1. Prayers--Fiction. 2. Baseball--Fiction. 3. Bears--Fiction. 4. Christian life--Fiction.] I. Berenstain, Stan, 1923- II. Berenstain, Jan, 1923- III. Title.
PZ7.B44827Bs 2008
[E]--dc22

2006032497

Editor: Betsy Flikkema
Art direction: Sarah Molegraaf

Printed in U.S.A.

09 10 11 • 9 8 7

My House
Sister

The Berenstain Bears®
Say Their Prayers

Created by Stan and Jan Berenstain
Written by Mike Berenstain

ZONDERkidz

ZONDERVAN.com/
AUTHORTRACKER
follow your favorite authors

It was bedtime in the Bear family's tree house—bedtime after a long, busy day. Little Honey Bear was already asleep in her crib. Brother and Sister were ready for bed too. They were bathed and they had their pajamas on. Mama and Papa were done reading them their bedtime stories. But there was one last thing to do before they went to sleep. It was time for Brother and Sister to kneel down beside their bunk bed and say their prayers.

"Bless Mama, bless Papa, bless Honey Bear, bless Grizzly Gramps, bless Grizzly Gran, bless Cousin Fred, Uncle Willie, and Aunt Min."

Some evenings, they added a few more blessings like "bless our friends Lizzy and Barry" or "bless Teacher Jane and Teacher Bob." But when they started adding "bless Mayor Honeypot and Police Chief Bruno," Mama and Papa decided to draw the line. Mama and Papa were falling asleep before the cubs' prayers were over.

Tonight when Mama and Papa were giving the cubs their goodnight kisses, Brother asked a question. It was a question he had been thinking about for awhile.

"Mama," he said. "Why do we say prayers before we go to sleep? I was at Barry Bruin's house for a sleepover last week, and he doesn't say prayers at all."

“Some people just don’t believe in saying prayers,” said Mama. “But we pray at night so we can thank God for the blessings of the day.”

“Do you and Papa always say your prayers before you go to sleep?” asked Sister, half asleep in the upper bunk.

“Not exactly …” said Mama. These days Mama and Papa were so tired at bedtime that they just flopped down and were snoring almost before their heads hit the pillow. “But I think it would be a good idea if we got in the habit again.” Mamma nudged Papa. “Don’t you agree, Papa?”

“Huh?” he said, trying to stay awake. “Oh, right! Absolutely!”

"Good night now," said Mama. "Sweet dreams."

"Hmmm ..." thought Brother, as he drifted off in the sleepy darkness. Mama's answer was okay. But he still had a few questions.

The next morning, Brother and Sister were up bright and early. It was Saturday and they had a Little League game. Their team was called the Sharks. They had a cool logo on their shirts—a big shark mouth full of sharp teeth.

"I feel hot today!" said Sister, tying her shoes. "I feel a whole lot of hits and stolen bases coming on!"

"Oh, yeah?" snorted Brother. "What about home runs? I guess I'll have to take care of that department!"

“Sure!” said Sister, punching him in the arm. “Brother Bear, the Home-Run King!” She ran, laughing, out of the room with Brother Bear chasing her. Sister and Brother liked playing on the same team. But sometimes they got just a little too competitive.

BEAR COUNTRY
CUB LEAGUE

After breakfast, the whole family headed down to the ball field. Brother and Sister had practice before the game. It was Mama and Papa's turn to help with the snack bar. Papa was going to cook the hamburgers and hot dogs on the grill. Mama was going to sell candy and popcorn. Even Honey Bear would help out. It was her job to eat the leftover cotton candy. Papa soon had the grill behind the snack bar fired up. Mama opened up the candy stand, and Honey Bear started getting into the cotton candy.

The team ran out on the field for practice. Brother was playing shortstop, and Sister was at second base. Up on the mound, Cousin Fred would handle the pitching. Fred was a solid pitcher. But he had been struggling of late. His last two games were pretty shaky.

Today, they were up against the Pumas. The Pumas' uniforms weren't quite as cool as the Sharks'. But the Pumas were one of the best teams in the league. The Sharks would have their work cut out for them.

Since the Sharks were the home team, the Pumas were up first. Their lead-off batter was a big, powerful cub about twice Brother's size. He was twirling six bats around his head in the warm-up circle as if they were a bunch of twigs.

"Uh-oh!" said Brother. "Look who it is!"

Sister gulped. It was the Beast—the Pumas' best player. He could hit and field and pitch. They didn't know his real name. They just called him the Beast.

Brother glanced over at Fred on the mound. He had noticed too. He was taking off his hat to wipe his forehead. He looked pretty nervous out there.

"Play ball!" called the ump, and the game was on.

The Beast picked out a bat from his bunch and stepped into the batter's box. He took some warm-up swings and pounded his bat on the plate. He glared at Fred on the mound.

Brother noticed that Fred wasn't glaring back. In fact, he was standing quite still, his head bowed and his hands folded. It looked like his eyes were closed, and his lips seemed to be moving.

"Psst, Fred!" called Brother. "What's up?"

But Fred didn't answer. He straightened up, took a deep breath, and went into his windup. He fired a fast ball. There was a *swish* and a *thump*! The Beast had missed!

"Stee-rike one!" called the ump.

"Way to go, Freddy baby!" yelled Brother. "That's the way to pitch 'em in there! Just two more like that! You can do it!"

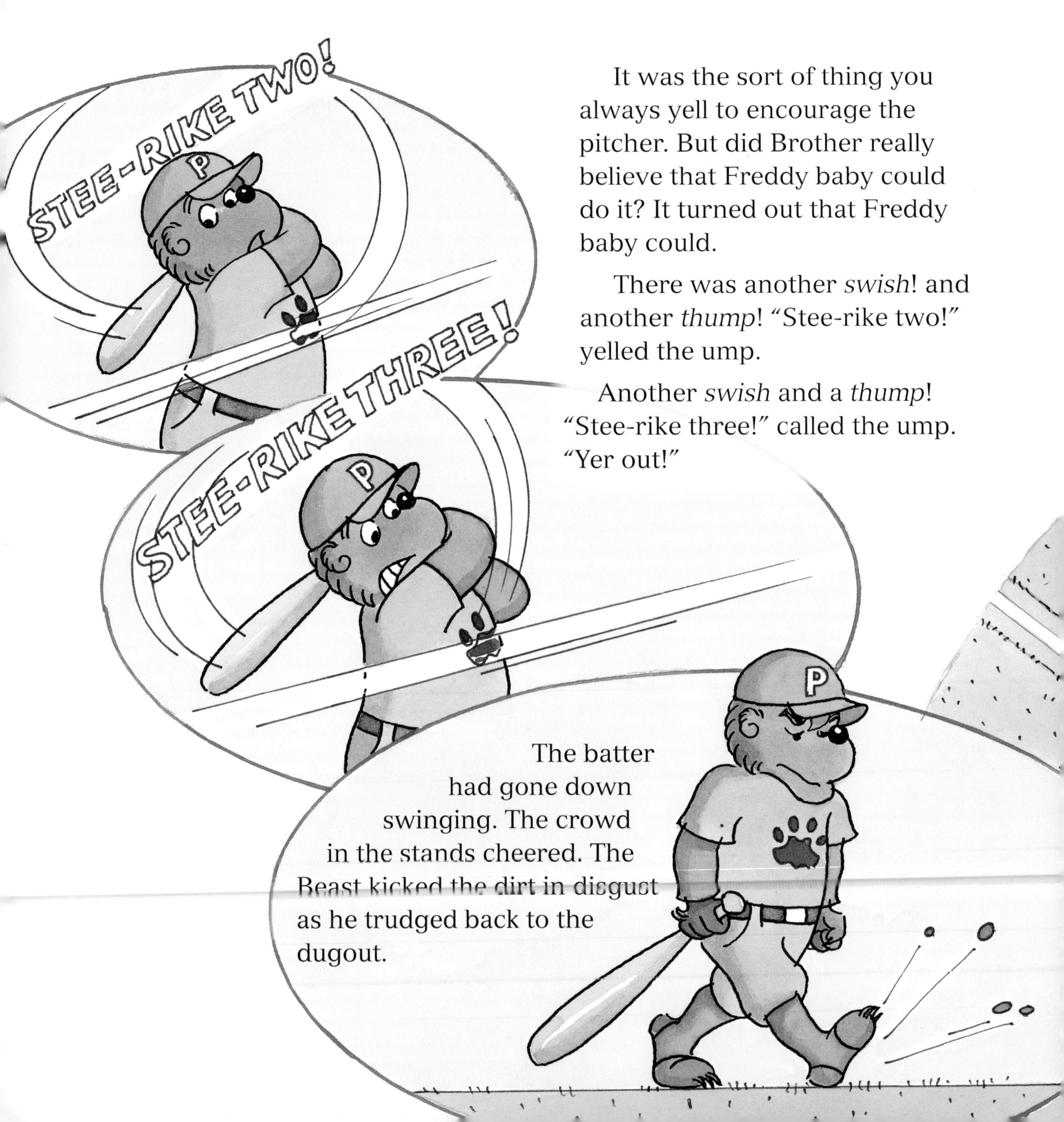

It was the sort of thing you always yell to encourage the pitcher. But did Brother really believe that Freddy baby could do it? It turned out that Freddy baby could.

There was another *swish*! and another *thump*! "Stee-rike two!" yelled the ump.

Another *swish* and a *thump*! "Stee-rike three!" called the ump. "Yer out!"

The batter had gone down swinging. The crowd in the stands cheered. The Beast kicked the dirt in disgust as he trudged back to the dugout.

Fred didn't look nervous anymore. Now it was the batter's turn to look nervous. Fred threw six more fast balls to two more batters. There were six *swishes* and six *thumps*. Cousin Fred had struck out the side!

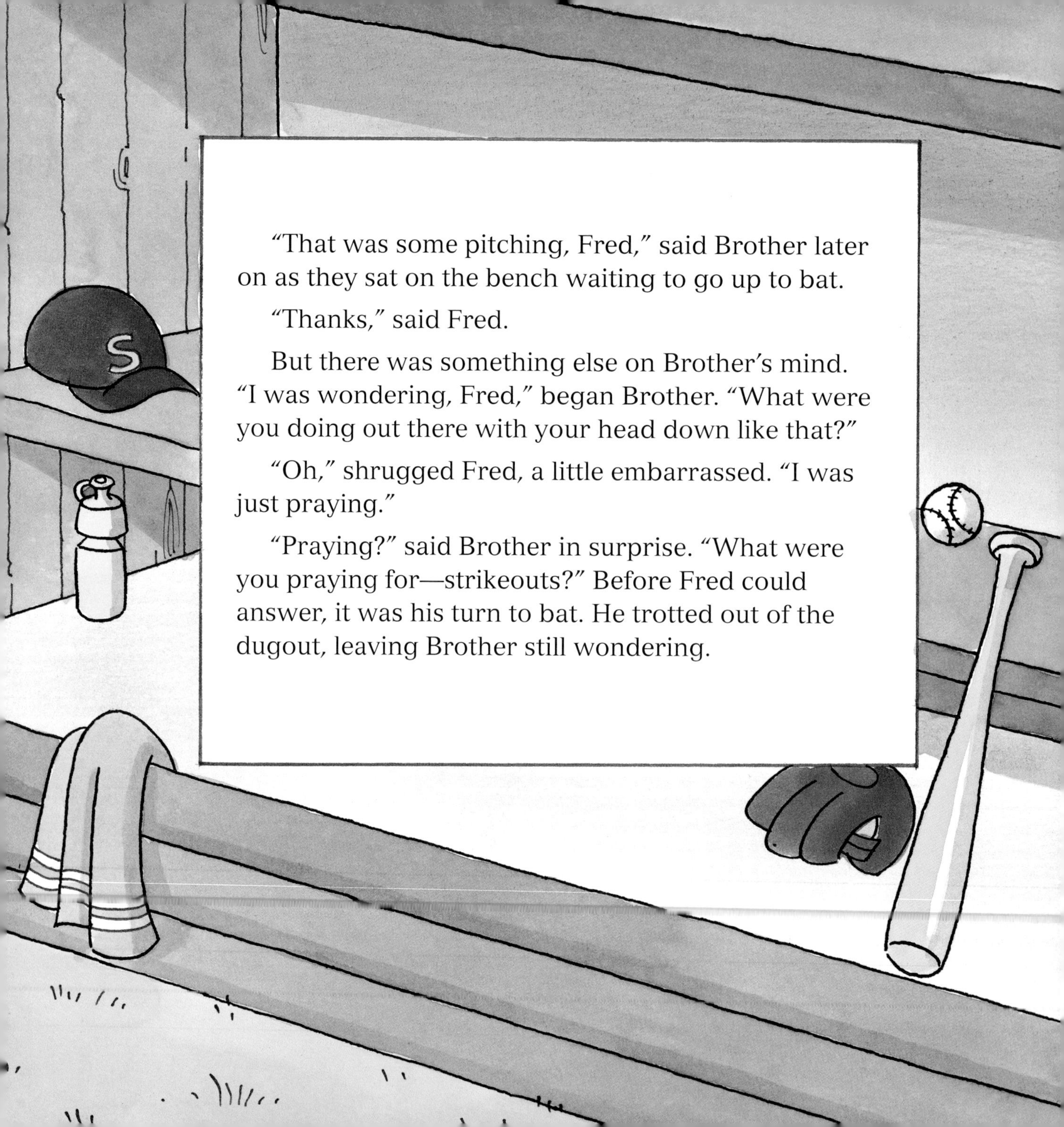

“That was some pitching, Fred,” said Brother later on as they sat on the bench waiting to go up to bat.

“Thanks,” said Fred.

But there was something else on Brother’s mind. “I was wondering, Fred,” began Brother. “What were you doing out there with your head down like that?”

“Oh,” shrugged Fred, a little embarrassed. “I was just praying.”

“Praying?” said Brother in surprise. “What were you praying for—strikeouts?” Before Fred could answer, it was his turn to bat. He trotted out of the dugout, leaving Brother still wondering.

S
BATTING ORDER
1. Barry Bruin 3B
2. Anna Grizzly LF
3. Cousin Fred P
4. Sister Bear 2B
5. Brother Bear SS
6. Lizzy Bruin RF
7. Millie Bruno CF
8. Harry McBear 1B
9. Bill

By the end of the game, Papa had cooked thirty-three hamburgers and forty-seven hot dogs; Mama had sold three dozen lollipops and four boxes of chocolate bars; and Honey Bear was very, very sticky.

The Sharks were in a sticky spot too. They were behind by one run with two outs and a man on base. The "man" was Sister. She had gotten to first on a walk and then stolen second—she was a feisty little player. Now it was Brother's turn to bat. If he could get a hit, the Sharks might tie it. If he got a home run, they would win.

The Pumas' pitcher was none other than the Beast. As he walked to the plate, Brother felt a little sick. Talk about pressure!

Before he stepped into the batter's box, Brother decided to do something he had never done in a baseball game. He bowed his head, closed his eyes, and said a prayer. "Dear Lord," he prayed. "Please let me get a hit."

Feeling a little more confident, Brother stepped up to the plate. The Beast wound up and let it fly. Brother didn't even see it.

"Stee-rike one!" called the ump.

Brother gripped the bat tighter. He'd get the next one. Another scorcher screamed past.

"Stee-rike two!" called the ump.

Brother clenched his teeth. He was definitely not going to let this next pitch get past him. The Beast wound up, the ball flew, and Brother swung—hard!

Swish!—Thump! "Stee-rike three!" bawled the ump. "Yer out!"

The game was over. The Sharks had lost, and Brother had struck out!

"Way to go, Home-Run King!" shouted Sister in disgust. She was angry that all her efforts to get on base had gone to waste. Brother trudged back to the dugout, his head hung low. He had never felt so awful in his life!

Later, as he packed up his things, he found Fred standing next to him. "Don't let it get to you, Brother," said Fred. "That was a tough game. The Pumas are a good team."

“Yeah,” agreed Brother. “I tried everything. I even tried praying like you did when you struck out the Beast. But it didn’t work for me.”

“Really?” said Fred. “What did you pray for?”

“I prayed for a hit, naturally,” said Brother.

“Oh,” said Fred, rubbing his chin. “I see.”

“Why?” asked Brother. “What did you pray for?”

“I just prayed that I wouldn’t get too scared,” said Fred simply.

Brother blinked at him. “I guess your prayer was answered!”

“Prayers are always answered,” said Fred. “Sometimes, we just don’t get the answer we expect. Say,” he added, sniffing the air. “Do you smell something burning?”

That's when they noticed the column of thick black smoke rising from behind the stands. "The snack bar!" they both yelled, and ran for it.

The smoke was coming from a batch of burning hot dogs on the grill. Papa was covered with soot and was trying to put the fire out with his hat. Mama came running up with a fire extinguisher. A few good squirts and the flames were under control. Honey Bear was laughing and clapping.

"Boy!" coughed Fred, waving the smoke away. "Maybe we should have prayed for rain!"

That evening at bedtime, Brother and Sister knelt down beside their bunk bed to say their prayers. Tonight, they felt like a nice long one:

When they were finished, Brother and Sister woke Mama and Papa up and climbed into bed. Mama and Papa kissed them goodnight, turned out the light, and went downstairs.

As Brother lay drowsily in his bed, he started thinking over the day's baseball game. If only he had been able to get that hit … or even a home run!

"That was a tough game today, wasn't it?" he said to Sister up on the top bunk.

"Yeah," answered Sister. "Tough on you, Mr. Strike-Out King."

"What's that supposed to mean?" said Brother, glaring up at the bottom of her bunk. "I played my best! A strike out like that could happen to anybody!"

But Sister didn't answer. She was fast asleep. Brother rolled over and ground his teeth. Sometimes Sister Bear made him so angry he could just ... But then he thought of something. He thought of another prayer.

"Dear God," he prayed. "Please help me out with my little sister!" And to his surprise, he found his prayer had been answered. He didn't feel angry anymore.

"Thanks for the help up there!" he said. And with a sigh, he fell asleep.